Scaredy Jake

ISBN 978-1-63885-283-4 (Paperback)
ISBN 978-1-63885-284-1 (Digital)

First Edition

Covenant Books, Inc.
11661 Hwy 707
Murrells Inlet, SC 29576
www.covenantbooks.com

Scaredy Jake

Paula Perdue

Jake did not have a home. He lived on the streets of the city. Life was not easy there. It was hard to find food and a place to sleep, and there were many scary things. Living on the streets was all Jake knew, but still, he felt like something was missing. *What could it be?* he thought.

There were many exciting things to do in the city, but Jake's favorite thing was chasing mice through the grass or cats up a tree. He would growl and bark, and he thought this was a good way to show the other stray dogs how tough and brave he was, but everyone really knew how brave Jake really was. That is why they called him Scaredy Jake.

Many things scared Jake, but what scared him the most were humans. Some of them were mean and threw things at him. Some of them chased him. Some of them seemed nice and would try to give him some food, but Jake was not taking any chances. The humans that scared him the most were the little ones. They were very loud and moved fast. Jake tried to stay away from humans.

One day, Jake was on the trail of a mouse and was not paying much attention to what was going on around him. Suddenly something was around his neck, and he could not get away. “Oh no,” he yelped. “There is a human on the other end of that thing.”

Dog
Warden

Jake began to shake. *What will I do now?* he thought. He tried to growl and bark, but it did not do any good. The next thing he knew, Jake was in a cage in a truck, and it was taking him away from everything he knew. He began to shake even more.

Jake was taken to the animal shelter. There he was put in another cage. This one was big and cold. *What is going to happen to me now?* he thought. The humans gave him food and water. They even tried to talk to him, but Jake decided he could not take any chances. He could not trust anyone.

The animal shelter housed many dogs and cats. Jake wondered if he would have to stay there forever. He did not like being in a cage, and he did not like being anywhere near humans. He was sad and very afraid.

The people at the animal shelter tried to get close to Jake, but he was too worried that something bad would happen to him. Whenever they tried to get close to him, he would bark and growl and shake. The people at the shelter decided Jake was too afraid to be around people, so they were not sure what to do with him.

One day, some people from a dog rescue place came to the animal shelter. They always looked at the "special dogs," the ones that were different or afraid. When they saw Jake, they decided to take him with them and put him up for adoption.

Meanwhile, there was a nice man and lady who lived in the country. They had adopted a dog named Chloe. Chloe loved humans. She would meet them at the door wagging her tail, and she would jump on their laps as soon as they sat down. Most of all, Chloe loved to play.

PetFinder

The nice man and lady thought it would be good for Chloe to have a playmate. They started looking for another dog. When they saw a picture of Jake, they decided to check him out. He was so cute, and he looked so sad. Maybe he would make a good playmate for Chloe.

The rescue place brought Jake to meet the family. *Oh no!* Jake thought. *Here we go again.* He was worried. *What will happen now?* He started to shake. The nice lady put out her hand to let Jake sniff it, and she talked to him in a soft and soothing voice. Something seemed different here. Jake was not sure what it was, but he began to relax a little.

Chloe looked up at Jake and wagged her tail. The rescue lady looked at Chloe and decided it was a good time for Jake and Chloe to meet. She put Jake on the floor. Chloe sniffed Jake and, in her doggy way, said, "Let's play." Off they went running through the house. Jake could not believe how nice Chloe was. *Could this be real?* he thought.

The nice man and lady took Chloe and Jake out to the backyard to play. Jake looked around and ran to the fence. He had climbed fences before in the city. Up and over he went, and off he ran.

As he ran, he could hear the nice lady calling him. Jake stopped. He could hear the worry in the nice lady's voice. *What should I do?* Jake thought. Jake turned and ran. He ran right into the nice lady's arms. She picked him up and snuggled him close. For the first time in his life, Jake felt safe and loved. Jake was home.

The End

About the Author

Growing up on a farm, author Paula Perdue always loved animals. As an adult, when choosing pets, she would choose to adopt a rescue animal or choose the so-called runt of the litter, because she believes all animals are special and have so much to offer. That is why she chose to write this story about her dog, Jake.

Paula also grew up very shy and had to learn to face fears in her life. God has taught her that sometimes one needs to step out of their comfort zone, and when they trust in God, all will be well.

CPSIA information can be obtained
at www.ICGtesting.com
Printed in the USA
LVHW070755291221
707423LV00007B/170